Glimmer

Madame Razz

Broom

The Sorceress

Queen Angella

Hardly anyone knows that Prince Adam of Eternia can use the Sword of Power to become He-Man, Master of the Universe – not even his mother and father!

But there is another sword in existence – the Sword of Protection – which also has magic powers. Here is the story of how the Sorceress sent Adam to find the owner of the Sword of Protection. He set off through a Time Gate and found himself in the land of Etheria, ruled by the evil Hordak and his minions, the Horde.

The owner surprisingly turned out to be Adora, Adam's twin sister, stolen as a baby from the King and Queen of Eternia!

And one last enormous surprise – the Sword of Protection turned Adora into Princess She-Ra, with all sorts of strange powers. But only He-Man and the Sorceress know of Adora's dual identity...

Designed by Stephen Pymm, using colour photographs from the film.

British Library Cataloguing in Publication Data

Daly, Audrey
    Secret of the sword.—(She-Ra Princess of Power; v. 3)
    I. Title   II. Series
    823'.914[J]   PZ7
    ISBN 0-7214-0978-4

First edition

Published by Ladybird Books Ltd Loughborough Leicestershire UK
Ladybird Books Inc Lewiston Maine 04240 USA

THE SECRET OF THE SWORD

story adaptation by Audrey Daly

Ladybird Books

In Castle Grayskull, deep in the heart of Eternia,
the Sorceress tossed in a troubled sleep, dreaming
of the past. Of Hordak, leader of the evil Horde that
menaced the land of Eternia. In her dream, she
saw him holding a baby girl in his arms.

"You may have defeated us," he was saying, "but
you'll never see this child again."

"Adora!" cried the Sorceress, and woke up,
weeping. Through her tears, she saw a sword
glowing in the air, beckoning her. She followed it
through the corridors until it stopped at a closed
door. Then suddenly the door burst open,
revealing a mysterious Time Gate glimmering at
the doorway. The sword fell to the floor.

"Can it be the Sword of Protection?" said the
Sorceress, picking it up. "After so long?"

*   *   *

Prince Adam was in the kitchens of the Royal
Palace of Eternia. He was baking spice bread,
watched by his pet tiger, Cringer. Suddenly he

heard the Sorceress calling him by telepathy.
Seconds later, he and Cringer stood beside her, in
front of the Time Gate.

"If this is a gate, where does it go to?" asked Adam.

"That I cannot say," said the Sorceress. "This door
has never opened before."

"You want me to pass through this gate and find
someone on the other side. And you can't tell me
who this person is?"

The Sorceress handed him the Sword of
Protection. "This sword will lead you to the one
you seek," she said.

"Why," said Adam, "except for the jewel in it, this
sword looks exactly like mine!"

"And like yours, it is intended for someone of a
special destiny," said the Sorceress.

Adam put it on his back, beside his own Sword of
Power. And he went forward, with Cringer,
through the Time Gate.

Now Adam and Cringer found themselves in the beautiful world of Etheria, ruled by the evil Horde. "There's an inn," said Adam, looking about him. "We might get food there."

Inside, a minstrel was playing his harp, and Bow the rebel sat in a corner, Kowl on his shoulder. "Do

you think he's a spy for the Horde, Kowl?" asked Bow.

"Unlikely," said Kowl, looking at Adam. "Hordesmen don't often smile."

The door slammed, and three troopers stalked in. Cringer dived under a table, and Bow's face grew grim. "Hordesmen!" he growled.

No one spoke as the Hordesmen sat down at a table. Then the minstrel began to play again. "I don't like that song!" said one of the Hordesman – and fired at the harp.

Adam was annoyed. He picked up the Hordesman and threw him into a barrel. Then Bow decided to help with the other two. As the fight raged from one side of the inn to the other, Kowl joined Cringer under the table.

When Bow and Adam had disposed of the three Hordesmen – one to a barrel – they shook hands. Kowl and Cringer crept out sheepishly.

"The Horde will send a Force Squad after us now," said Kowl.

Bow nodded. "You'd better come with us to Whispering Woods, Adam, and help with our great Rebellion."

In the main hall of Doom Tower, in the Fright Zone, a messenger was speaking. "Mighty Hordak, I bring you bad news from the village of Thaymor in Bright Moon. Three of our troopers were defeated by two rebels."

Shadow Weaver glided up with more bad news. "A stranger from another world has come to Etheria, bringing with him the seeds of great trouble for the Horde. He is somewhere in the Kingdom of Bright Moon, but my spells can no longer find him."

"Bright Moon!" hissed Catra, standing near.
"Could *he* have beaten our troopers, Hordak?"

"You may be right, Catra," said Hordak. He
shouted to a Hordesman, "Send Force Captain
Adora to me at once."

Then he spoke to the villains around him. "We
will teach this stranger it's not nice to cause trouble
for the Evil Horde!"

Meanwhile, Bow had taken Adam into Whispering Woods to meet Glimmer, leader of the rebels. She was the daughter of Queen Angella, who had once ruled Bright Moon. On the way to the camp Adam also met Sprag, one of the Twiggets who lived in the Woods.

Just as Bow was telling Glimmer that he and Adam had taught three Hordesmen a lesson in the village of Thaymor, Madame Razz flew in with Broom. She had news. A Horde Force Captain and four villains had arrested everyone in the village of Thaymor because of the fight at the inn.

"If the culprits don't give themselves up, Hordak says he will send the whole village to the mines as slaves."

"He'd do it, too, the fiend," said Glimmer.

"Surely we can save the village without giving ourselves up," said Adam. "I've a friend who might help," he added quietly.

Glimmer looked at Sprag and the peasant rebels nearby, and they nodded.

"All right then, let's save Thaymor!" she cried. And everyone cheered.

At that very moment, the villagers were being loaded into the Horde Slave Transporter.

Catra and the three other Horde villains, standing by their Horde Flyers, were grumbling. "If Force Captain Adora wasn't Hordak's favourite, she wouldn't be in charge and we wouldn't have to do as she says," said Leech. Mantenna was very unhappy. "That's right," he said. "We could have some fun destroying the village."

Then there was a shout. "For Bright Moon! Attack!" It was Glimmer leading the little band of rebels to the rescue.

The Hordesmen were taken by surprise, but they soon recovered. The rebels were few, and the villains soon began to gain the upper hand in the battle. When Adam saw this happening, he decided that it was time for He-Man to help. "By the Power of Grayskull!" he called and raised the Sword of Power. Seconds later, he *was* He-Man – and his cowardly cat had become Battle-Cat.

The fight began all over again. He-Man and Battle-Cat fought hard, and to start with, they were winning. Then Mantenna's beam hit He-Man, and he fell. The beam was destroying his sense of

balance! He managed to get to his feet, but then he found that Force Captain Adora was firing at him. He flung his sword at her, smashing her blaster, and she turned to run. When he caught up with her, she had her back to the wall, her sword out.

He-Man pulled out the Sword of Protection, and broke Adora's weapon with one swift move. As he did so, he saw to his amazement that the Sword of Protection was glowing. He lowered it, puzzled. "You must be the one I came to find," he said.

"Is that so?" said Adora, smiling cruelly as she watched a Hordesman taking aim at He-Man. He fired and as He-Man fell to the ground, Adora said, "You're mine now, stranger. You – and this curious sword."

Back at the rebel camp, Madame Razz and three of the Twiggets were holding hands in a circle round a little tree. Madame Razz was casting a spell, and Glimmer and Bow were watching anxiously, along with Battle-Cat.

"I hope Madame's spell can find He-Man," whispered Glimmer to Bow.

Suddenly a picture formed at the top of the little tree. "Dearie me," said Madame Razz. "It's Beast Island!"

"I've heard rumours that the Horde have a prison there," said Bow.

"If that's where He-Man is," said Battle-Cat, "let's go."

Madame Razz started on another spell, but it went wrong. At last she managed to magic a flying ship just above the trees. Glimmer transported herself aboard, and helped the others up, and they set off for Beast Island.

For once Madame Razz hadn't got it wrong at all.
He-Man *was* on Beast Island – imprisoned on a
huge slab of stone by electro-bonds.

Force Captain Adora was standing beside him,
the Sword of Protection in her hand. "I'm Force
Captain Adora," she said, swishing the blade
through the air. "This sword feels as if it were
made just for me."

"I'm He-Man," said her prisoner. "I thought the
sword was for you when it glowed. But I was to
give that sword to someone who served good. And
you serve evil!"

"*You're* the one who serves evil, rebel. I serve the Horde, the rightful rulers of Etheria."

"You *must* have seen how the Horde treats people," said He-Man.

"I've spent most of my life training in the Fright Zone," said Adora. "I don't know much about the rest of Etheria."

"You should go and find out. Or are you afraid to?" taunted He-Man.

"I'm afraid of nothing!" said Adora. "But I'll think about it."

She put the sword back in its sheath, and walked thoughtfully away.

On Madame Razz's flying ship, Glimmer and Bow were keeping watch. Kowl perched beside them on the rail.

"Beast Island!" Glimmer said suddenly, pointing downwards.

As everyone came to peer down, Bow said, "Oh, oh! We've got trouble!"

It was Hordak in his Annihilator, on his way to the prison; Shadow Weaver sat beside him.

He smiled nastily as he saw them and punched a button. Seconds later the little flying ship fell out of the sky. Its mast and sail had gone, smashed by a ball of pulsating energy from Hordak's cannons. The Horde leader grinned and flew on into the prison.

*   *   *

Flames roared and licked at the crashed ship. Surely no one could still be alive. Or could they? A glowing bubble of light emerged from the fire – Glimmer's magic powers were holding the rebels safe within its circle.

Everyone gathered round as she sank to the ground, exhausted. Kowl watched her, worried. "The Horde might send men here," he said. "Better to leave this area immediately."

"I'll carry her," said Battle-Cat. Bow helped Glimmer into the saddle, and they set off once more to rescue He-Man.

Inside the prison, Shadow Weaver was praising Adora. "You have served the Horde well by capturing this stranger," said Shadow Weaver.

"His name is He-Man," said Adora.

"*I'm* proud of you too, Adora," said Hordak.

"Thank you, Mighty One," said Adora. "May I return to the Fright Zone now? I have to do some investigating."

"Of course," said Hordak. "Go."

As Adora left, Shadow Weaver said, "There's something here I don't understand. She should be watched."

Hordak brushed her words aside. Adora had always been a favourite of his. "She's loyal enough. The spells you have put on her make sure of that."

* * *

Madame Razz and the little band of rebels were still having a bad time as they struggled through the jungle on their way to the prison. One of the terrible beasts after which the islands was named came after them, shrieking its rage. First Battle-Cat then Bow tried to stop it, without success. Madame Razz tried to magic it away – but she got the spell wrong, as she so often did.

The rest ran for their lives, but the monster landed right on top of Bow. But Battle-Cat had a surprise in store. Before the monster could make another move, it was hit by one juicy fruit after another. Bow and Battle-Cat fled as the monster tried to clear its eyes to see. "Thanks, Battle-Cat!" said Bow.

*   *   *

Shadow Weaver's doubts had been right! Adora had dressed in the clothes of an Etherian peasant and had gone out on her horse Spirit. She was going to see just how the Horde *did* treat the Etherians. He-Man *must* be wrong!

As she rode out through one gate – telling the sentry she was on a secret mission for Hordak – the rebels went in through another gate. Bow and Glimmer had overcome the guards and taken their uniforms.

They were unlucky once more, however. From the moment they arrived at the prison, Grizzlor had been watching on a viewscreen. Now he pressed a button, and the doors near the rebels slid shut. A ray projector beamed in and everyone cowered away. Then Bow shot an arrow up the

narrow barrel, and the projector exploded. Battle-
Cat smashed a door down, and the rebels started to
look for He-Man again.

But Grizzlor still had an eye on them – and he
told Hordak they were there!

*   *   *

Meantime, Adora was out in the Fright Zone,
watching and listening. She saw slaves in a Horde
slave caravan being ill-treated by the cruel
troopers. Whips were flourished to hurry the slaves
along, and when one old man asked for water, he
was flung in a pool.

Later, she saw a peasant's house blown up – just
because he said the Horde's taxes were too high.

Adora was growing very unhappy. It looked as if
He-Man was right!

   While Adora was out learning the truth, the
rebels had found He-Man. But Hordak, Grizzlor and
Shadow Weaver had been waiting for them.
Shadow Weaver paralysed Bow, Glimmer, Madame
Razz and Broom with magic smoke. Battle-Cat was
tied up, unable to move. There was no sign of
Kowl.

   "Welcome to Beast Island, rebels!" said Hordak.

   He-Man was struggling once more to get free of
his electro-bonds. "You villain! What have you done
to them?"

"They are merely out of action for a time. Better to ask what I *will* do to them if you do not tell me why you have come to Etheria!"

He-Man was silent. After a moment, Grizzlor took the rebels off to a cell, and Hordak said, "We will give you time to think. Come, Shadow Weaver."

As the two villains went off, Kowl flapped down from where he had been hiding. "Can you get me loose?" said He-Man.

"Certainly," said Kowl. "Give me a moment." He flapped off to the control console, and started to peck at the buttons. All of a sudden the force field faded, and He-Man sat up.

"Let's go find our friends," he said to Kowl. "I've had enough of this place!"

Now He-Man went into action. He pulled the door off the rebels' cell and said, "Time to go, folks!"

Glimmer was worried. "We have to get to one of the Horde Flyers. It's the only way off the island."

"I believe the Horde's landing pad is to our right," said Kowl.

They set off – but it wasn't going to be quite so easy. As they came out on to the landing pad, Grizzlor came straight for them in a destructo tank, all cannons firing. He-Man waited until it was almost on him, then he raised his fist in one mighty punch. The tank fell to pieces, and Grizzlor hit the ground, a stunned expression on his face.

"Come on, He-Man!" yelled Glimmer. All the others were inside a Flyer, anxious to return to Whispering Woods.

"I've one more job to do. Take off and wait," said He-Man.

And as they watched from a safe distance, He-Man pulled and heaved and cracked off the whole mountain top. Then he dropped it on the prison.

The Flyer picked him up, and as he got in, He-Man said, "That's one prison the Horde will have to do without!"

Hordak was now back in the Fright Zone, in his own quarters. He was talking to Shadow Weaver. "This He-Man is too dangerous to us. We must find out why he is here. And how we can stop him."

As he spoke, Adora came in. The Sword of Protection was in her hand, and she pointed it at them both.

"I've been seeing for myself how we rule Etheria," she said. "You lied to me. The Horde is evil, cruel, unjust, and the people hate us." She was angry, but she was also confused. Hordak had always been her hero.

Shadow Weaver whispered to Hordak, "My spell on her has weakened. It has something to do with that sword she holds."

"Then you must strengthen the spell," said Hordak.

Shadow Weaver glided over to Adora, who swung the sword towards her. "Stay away!"

"Surely you would not harm me, Adora. Am I not like a mother to you?" asked Shadow Weaver. She suddenly waved her hand across Adora's face, casting a spell on her.

"Sleep…" said Shadow Weaver softly, and Adora crumpled to the floor.

"First this He-Man arrives, and now Adora turns against me," said Hordak.

"Remember who she really is," said Shadow Weaver.

"Yes," said Hordak, pondering. "Yes…"

"I must find out the secrets of this sword," said Shadow Weaver, looking at it. "And those of He-Man as well."

Hordak looked thoughtfully across at her, then they both began to laugh wickedly.

The rebels were now safely back in Whispering Woods and He-Man had become Adam once more. Glimmer was arguing with him. "You'll be captured for certain if you go back to the Fright Zone, Adam."

"Sorry, Glimmer, I've a mission that must be performed, safe or not," said Adam.

He looked down at Cringer. "You'll have to stay here, Cringer. You're too noticeable."

He said goodbye to the rebels and left.

*   *   *

On the roof of Doom Tower, Hordak was admiring a huge ray machine. He turned to Shadow Weaver and Adora. "At last it is finished – a thing of beauty! It's my new Magna Beam Transporter. See that old battlewaggon? I don't

need it any more, so…"
Hordak pressed a button,
and the battlewaggon
shimmered for a moment
then vanished.

"Where did it go?"
asked Mantenna.

"Look!" said Hordak,
pointing to the
viewscreen. "It's gone to
the Valley of the Lost —
no one ever returns from
there. When my Magna
Beam is at full power, I
shall send all the rebels there and we'll have no
more trouble. Let's go down to the Plunder Room,
and I'll show you how we will charge it up."

Down in the Plunder Room, Hordak told his
villains that will power — and a lot of it — was needed
to charge up the Magna Beam. The guards locked a

prisoner into the
Magna Beam Booth,
and everyone watched.
The prisoner was
defiant to start with,
but gradually fell silent,
completely drained.

Hordak looked at the
Magna Beam indicator.
"Bah! He'd less will
power than I'd hoped!
We must capture more
rebels."

*   *   *

Unfortunately for Adam, he too was on his way to the Magna Beam Booth, although he didn't yet know it. He had transformed into He-Man, then captured a Horde trooper and put his uniform on.

But Shadow Weaver and Hordak saw him on the viewscreen. They knew him at once. "He would be a source of great power," said Shadow Weaver. "All the energy we need."

As He-Man marched into the Fright Zone, he suddenly saw Adora, and hurried to her.

"How did *you* get here?" she gasped.

She started to draw her stun pistol, and he stopped her.

"You don't need that," he said. "You must know about the Horde by now."

"What I know is that you are a lying rebel spy!" she said, her face hardening, under Shadow Weaver's spell. "And you are under arrest."

Now Hordak arrived with some guards. He-Man put up a good fight, but he was soon overpowered. And then – there he was, in the Magna Beam Booth!

During the night, as He-Man's strength slowly drained away, Adora tossed and turned in her sleep. She muttered from time to time, "No, no, it's evil..."

Then through Adora's dreams, the Sorceress called softly, "Adora... Adora..." and she woke up.

After a moment Adora said, "Something strange is happening. I must find out what it is."

She went straight to the Plunder Room. He-Man lay slumped in the booth – and the Magna Beam indicator stood at 'full'. The two great swords were on a pedestal nearby.

"Everything seems in order," said Adora. Then she looked almost sadly at He-Man. "The strong rebel grows weaker – but it is for the good of the Horde. Why do I feel so unsure?"

She turned to go – and the gem in the Sword of Protection suddenly glowed, startling her. The Sorceress's face floated in the glow. "It's time to throw off the Horde's spell, Adora. Use this sword to help you to right wrongs and protect the weak. But first, you must save He-Man."

"A rebel?" asked Adora, confused.

"He is no rebel. He is a champion of goodness. But... he is also your twin brother! The Horde stole you when you were a baby..." Her voice faded. "For the honour of Grayskull, Adora..."

Adora slowly raised the Sword of Protection. "For the Honour of Grayskull," she repeated. Then...

"I am She-Ra," she cried – and smashed the Magna Beam Booth.

He-Man lifted his head weakly. "Who are you?" he asked.

"A friend," said She-Ra.

He looked across at the Sword of Power. "My sword..."

Suddenly understanding, She-Ra tossed it to him. His strength flooded back and he cried, "I have the power!" Then he turned to She-Ra. "Let's get out of here."

It was too late. Hordak had arrived on the scene. First he looked at the Magna Beam indicator. "My Beam is fully charged!" he said, pleased. Then, "I don't know who you are," he said to She-Ra, "but your rescue is too late. Guards, arrest these two rebels. I'm going upstairs to take care of the rest of the rebels with my Magna Beam." With that, he went away.

"What is this Magna Beam?" asked He-Man.

"Don't ask!" said She-Ra. "We must stop him."

"I'll take care of that," said He-Man. "You go and warn the Rebellion."

As He-Man started to fight off the guards, She-Ra turned and made for the stable and her horse, Spirit. But as she climbed on his back he became Swift Wind, a winged unicorn, carrying She-Ra to warn the rebels.

Now He-Man was going after Hordak. He found him on the Fright Zone roof, just switching on the Magna Beam. But She-Ra had looked back as she flew away, and had seen what was happening. She found a huge rock and threw it into the path of the beam. Both rock and beam disappeared instantly!

Hordak was furious. "My Magna Beam – wasted! Well, I still have some power left, to try again."

But He-Man had other ideas. He gave the machine a mighty punch – and split it down the middle. As it split, an enormous burst of energy was released. The energy spread outwards from the ruined

Magna Beam, and when it reached the Horde's prisoners, it gave them their will power back. Without wasting a moment they broke out and went back to Whispering Woods to help the Rebellion.

Hordak was white with rage. "I've still got you, rebel. I'm going to freeze you solid with freeze rays..."

But he was wrong again. She-Ra swooped down on Swift Wind, and lifted He-Man to safety – just in time.

"Thanks!" said He-Man.

"No problem," said She-Ra. "What are sisters for anyway?"

"Sister?" said He-Man, puzzled.

She-Ra smiled. "He-Man, I think we've a lot to talk about!" she said.

* * *

Deep in Whispering Woods, Swift Wind shone white in the moonlight. She-Ra stroked him while He-Man was speaking. "I don't understand. You're my sister? But I never had a sister."

"I didn't know I had a brother until the woman in the sword told me so!" said She-Ra.

"The sword!" said He-Man. "It must be the Sorceress!" He lifted the Sword of Protection and called, "Sorceress, can you hear me?"

Its jewel gleamed, and the Sorceress spoke. "Now, I can answer all your questions...

"Years ago, twins were born to the King and Queen of Eternia. One of these babies was you, Adam, and the other was Adora. The king and queen were delighted, but their joy soon turned to sorrow.

"A terrible force called the Horde, led by a fiend called Hordak, tried to conquer Eternia."

The Sorceress paused, looking back. "But they were no match for King Randor and my magic, and we defeated them.

"Then Hordak with his favourite pupil Skeletor decided to steal both the queen's babies in revenge.

But they got only Adora, because Man-at-Arms caught the villains in the act.

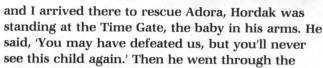

"Hordak escaped with Adora, but Skeletor was caught and told us the way to Hordak's secret base.

"When Man-at-Arms and I arrived there to rescue Adora, Hordak was standing at the Time Gate, the baby in his arms. He said, 'You may have defeated us, but you'll never see this child again.' Then he went through the

Time Gate. We never told Adam about you, Adora, because no matter how we searched, we couldn't find you." There the Sorceress's story ended.

As the Sorceress's voice faded, She-Ra looked troubled. "But I can't just leave Etheria and go back to Eternia. The Rebellion needs me!"

"You will have to think things over," said He-Man. "Now, how about giving your brother a big hug?"

* * *

He-Man and She-Ra became Adam and Adora once more as they heard voices nearby in the Woods. It was Bow and Glimmer arguing. They were startled to see Adam and Adora, and still more surprised to learn that Adora was Adam's sister.

"I'm with the Rebellion now," said Adora. "I was only serving the Horde because of Shadow Weaver's evil spell. Anyway, what's the argument about? Can we help?"

"My mother, Queen Angella, was the last ruler of Bright Moon. I've just found out she's a slave to Hunga, the leader of the Harpies of Talon Mountain. We must rescue her, but Bow thinks it's too dangerous," said Glimmer.

"We can do that better than you," said Adora. "Just leave it to us. Let's go, Adam." And as soon as they were out of sight, they became She-Ra and He-Man.

*   *   *

As Swift Wind dipped towards Talon Mountain, He-Man and She-Ra on his back, Hunga the Harpy was watching on a viewscreen. Near her, Queen Angella was chained to the floor. "We have visitors," said Hunga. "Let us prepare a surprise!"

44

So when She-Ra and He-Man burst in and raced over to free Angella from her chains, it turned out to be Hunga the Harpy in disguise! Her force beams threw them to the floor to start with,

then she used her magic to put a cage round them.

He-Man and She-Ra grinned at each other, and brought their own magic into play. First they destroyed the cage, then they went after the queen Harpy. She was soon tied up and gagged.

They found Queen Angella and set her free.

"Come on," said He-Man. "Your daughter Glimmer wants to see you."

The rebels started to cheer – and went on cheering – as Queen Angella arrived. When she put her arms round her daughter Glimmer, they were both so happy they burst into tears.

She-Ra turned to He-Man. "I was thinking. With Queen Angella back, the rebels will have a much better chance. I could go and see *my* mother and father in Eternia!"

As Adam and Adora, they set off on Spirit, with Cringer loping alongside.

"There's one thing, Adora," said He-Man. "Mother and Father don't know I'm He-Man. And you mustn't tell them you're She-Ra, either."

As he was speaking, two Horde troopers saw them riding by. "That's Force Captain Adora!" said one. "We must tell Hordak!"

Just as Adora and Adam were going through the Time Gate, Hordak arrived to see Adora disappearing. "She's not going to escape me!" he howled. And transforming to his rocket shape, he went through the gate after her.

* * *

On the other side of the Time Gate, in Castle Grayskull, the Sorceress said, "Welcome back to Eternia, princess."

Adora looked puzzled. "Princess?"

"You *are* the daughter of a king and queen, remember!" smiled Adam.

Then the Sorceress raised her hands, and the little party disappeared once more – to find themselves in the Royal Palace of Eternia. When the king and queen realised that Adora was their long-lost daughter, they could hardly speak for joy. Even Man-at-Arms brushed away a tear as he told Teela, "She's Adam's twin sister – and she's back. After all this time."

*   *   *

When Hordak first went through the Time Gate and realised he was on Eternia, he made for Skeletor's hideout in Snake Mountain.

Skeletor wasn't pleased to see Hordak again, and they began a tremendous fight. Hordak called a halt first. "It's stupid to fight like this," he said. "I'm only here to recapture Princess Adora, daughter of King Randor. Help me to get her back, and I'll leave you in peace."

"You don't frighten me, Hordak," said Skeletor. "But I'll help you, if only to get rid of you." Then he laughed wickedly. "I've just thought of a plan."

"Why, it'll be just like the old days!" chuckled Hordak.

*   *   *

The villains' plan worked. The royal family was having dinner when an enormous cake was wheeled in by three cooks. The cooks were really

Skeletor and his villains – and Hordak was *inside* the cake. They took everyone by surprise. Adora was captured very quickly and taken to Snake Mountain. There she faced the Time Gate with Hordak.

But Skeletor's idea was different. His villains threw Hordak through the Gate – and Adora was taken to the dungeons.

This was her chance! Adora escaped, found her sword, and transformed to She-Ra. Fighting her way out, she met He-Man, Teela, Man-at-Arms and Battle-Cat, who were on their way to rescue Adora. "The princess is safe," she told them.

When Snake Mountain grew quiet again, Skeletor could be heard saying feebly, "A female He-Man! This is the worst day of my life!"

Back in the royal palace, Adora had sad news for the king and queen.

"I'm afraid I must go back to Etheria, to help against the Horde," she said. "I will come home to you once more when my world is free."

"We wish you would stay," said King Randor. "But we understand, and we're proud of you."

*　　*　　*

The moment Adora went through the Time Gate, she sensed there was trouble afoot. So she was glad to find she wasn't alone. Adam had come through the Time Gate behind her.

They looked up to see the sky filled with Horde Flyers, and with one accord, they transformed. He-Man on Battle-Cat, and She-Ra on Swift Wind, raced to join up with the rebels.

On the way, She-Ra discovered she had yet more strange powers. She was even able to ask some of

the animals to help in the fight to put Queen
Angella back on the throne of Bright Moon.

Hordak laughed as he saw the rebels moving in
to attack the Castle. Within seconds, he threw
planes, tanks, stun cannons and troops into action
against them.

Then He-Man and She-Ra came into the
fight – and Hordak's laughter stopped.

Not long after that, the rebels entered Castle
Bright Moon. Queen Angella was back on the
throne, and Hordak and his minions were defeated.

*   *   *

He-Man went back to Eternia – but She-Ra stayed
behind. As herself or as Adora, Etheria needed her
help. And if ever extra help were needed, He-Man
would return.

Doom Tower

Hordak

Shadow
Weaver

Skeletor